Sentry Books
An imprint of Great West Publishing

Library of Congress Control Number: 2007938941
ISBN: 978-0-9796199-1-5

Illustrations by Susana Sayles
Cover artwork by Susana Sayles and Sarah Garibaldi
Book design and layout by Jonathan Gullery

Printed in the United States of America

THE ARBORIST

BY

M.S. HOLM

Great West Publishing
USA

For

My Mother and Father

I

MY SISTER IRENE SAID it was the ugliest Christmas tree she had ever seen, but I didn't care. You only needed imagination to see what it could become.

I found it at the back of Mr. Paulson's tent. My father, Irene, and I had gone there to buy our tree. It stood by itself in the corner with its top chopped off and orange sap oozing from the end. The branches were lopsided, and the trunk was crooked. You could see white wounds where the bark had been skinned.

Irene laughed when she saw me checking it out.

"No roadkill, please," she said.

As usual, my sister had picked out the tallest tree in the tent, a perfect Douglas fir so full and triangular that it could have stood in the White House.

While my dad tied it to the roof of our minivan, I remained in the tree tent, breathing the piney smell and staring at the puny tree in the corner.

"Is this one for sale?" I asked Mr. Paulson.

"Why, it's just a lop-off, Charlie," he said. "Going to make a wreath, are you?"

"I don't know," I replied, but I knew exactly what I was going to do with it.

"Here," he said, picking it up with one hand. He held it out as if he might twirl it. "No charge."

When I carried it out of the tent, Irene protested.

"Don't bring that thing near here! It's probably got tree rabies or something."

I leaned it against our car.

"Trees don't get rabies," I answered.

"Dad! I don't want our tree catching whatever that sick one has!"

My dad said, "That's enough, you two. We'll put it in the back."

And that's the beauty of our Plymouth minivan. A normal tree fits inside.

On our way home, Irene announced, "I'm not getting within a mile of that thing."

I kept my mouth shut. The needles of my puny tree tickled me from across the rear seat. A mile was fine with me. Actually, a mile was pretty close. Irene could never have guessed that my ugly tree was going to Chief Goodyear.

I was the first kid to spot him from the school bus when he showed up in town that September.

"Hey! Who's that?" I said one morning, pointing to a stranger sitting on a stack of tires in the vacant lot next to Hildreth's Hardware. He was holding a pan over a fire.

In our town, you didn't see strangers cooking in public like that, so kids glued their faces to the bus window. In the same corner of the lot, we saw a homemade tent that looked like a tepee.

"Why is he camped in our lot?" asked Gooter.

Gooter and I are best buddies, but he's a lot more territorial than me. In the summer, we played baseball and soccer at Hildreth's lot. In the winter, we built forts and waged snowball wars there.

"He must be living there," I answered.

The next day and the day after that, we saw him again. By the end of the week, rumors ran the length of the bus. Some kids said he was a hobo from the yards; others guessed he was an illegal alien. Gooter started calling him Chief Goodyear because of the tepee and his seat made of tires. Then the name stuck.

When my father drove us to church on Sunday morning, Chief Goodyear was still there. My mom noticed.

"Harold, did you see that?" she asked, looking back.

As a rule, my dad never took his eyes off the road when he was behind the wheel.

"See what?" he replied.

"A man is living in a tent next to Hildreth's."

"He's been there all week," I interjected, trying to be helpful. "I saw him from the bus."

"Maybe we should call the police," said Irene.

Of course, Irene would say something like that!

"I wonder what he's doing there," my mom remarked.

On the way home after church, my dad slowed the Plymouth in front of Hildreth's Hardware.

Chief Goodyear was busy near his tepee. His gray hair stuck out in every direction, and his clothes were dirty and ruffled like he had been sleeping in them.

Suddenly, he turned and looked at us. His face was friendly. He smiled and waved.

My parents jerked back like they had just spotted an alien. Then they lifted their hands and wagged them stiffly. I gave a big wave. Irene didn't move.

"We should report him," she whispered.

"He's not bothering anybody," I said.

"What if he's crazy? What if he's a fugitive?"

"Irene, please," said my mom.

"I wonder if he's one of the people from the hurricane," my dad muttered.

"Poor man."

"Let's get out of here," said Irene. "He gives me the creeps."

"Maybe we should help him. Bring him food or something," I suggested.

"We'll see," said my mom.

"He'll probably be gone in a few days," said my dad as we left the lot behind.

I watched Chief Goodyear return to his tent. Then I waved again.

The next week, I watched from the bus every day, expecting to see Chief Goodyear gone and our lot vacant again. The word from the back of the bus, where all the high school kids sat, was that the police were going to arrest him. Our driver said that Mr. Hildreth would run him off.

But on Friday, the stranger was still camped in the corner, and he now had a grill. It wasn't much of a grill. It was more like a bowl with legs, but it was smoking.

"The chief is putting down roots," said Gooter. "Someone ought to tell him that's our lot."

On Saturday, I rode my Mongoose BMX to Hildreth's to buy kite string and glue. Because I was in the neighborhood, I stopped by the lot. I just can't resist a closer look when a phenomenon is in town.

As soon as I got off my bike, I spotted the small, black dog near the tent. At first, I thought it was a stray sniffing out the chief's campsite. Then I saw it was tied to the tent.

"Hello there," I said in a friendly voice.

He gave me a perky-eared look, then lay down next to the tent and closed his eyes. I couldn't see the stranger anywhere, though immediately I noticed how clean the lot looked. Trash had been picked up, and the big stones we used to mark corner kicks and foul lines had been gathered into piles along the walls. The area around the tent looked swept. Naturally, I wondered if the stranger had something to do with these improvements. Had Mr. Hildreth decided to put him to work instead of running him off?

Of course, I didn't think twice about giving the place a tour. After all, it was our lot. Mr. Hildreth had practically signed it over.

I wandered in the direction of Chief Goodyear's stack of tires. A stone held down a piece of cardboard that covered the tire holes. I held my breath and raised one corner of the cardboard, peeking in from as far away as I could. You never know what you're going to find at the bottom of a stack of tires when a man sits on them in a vacant lot. What I saw was a bag of charcoal, another bag of dry dog food, and a can of lighter fluid. This must be the Chief's pantry. I let out my breath.

Nearby, the smell of burnt food reached me from the grill. I edged toward it for a closer look, but the dog suddenly jumped up and began to bark. The next moment, he was tugging on his leash in high alert.

"Not the grill," he seemed to be saying. "Not the grill!"

Then I froze. Something had stirred in the tent. Someone was inside! Before I could retreat, a pair of legs snaked from the opening. Wild, gray hair appeared, and I immediately recognized the owner.

Chief Goodyear stood. He looked at his dog and then at me.

"Shush, Pipe," he said to the dog.

"Welcome," he said to me.

"Don't talk to strangers," a little voice in my head said. It was my mom's number-one rule. Unless I wanted my picture tacked to the post office bulletin board with the word "Missing" above it, I was supposed to obey this rule while I was out and about.

"Hi, mister," I replied.

After watching him from the bus for two weeks, Chief Goodyear just didn't seem like a stranger anymore.

"I was only looking," I added quickly. I didn't want him to think that I was a spy or stalker or someone up to no good.

The chief glanced at his tent and said, "I'm afraid there isn't much to look at."

The dog dropped his bark for a low, throaty growl. He sounded like my dad's chainsaw on idle. I watched him turn on himself, tugging at his own fur.

"Pipe, hush," the chief warned again.

The little dog stopped.

"That's a funny name for a dog," I said.

"Isn't it?" he agreed. "I pulled him from a flooded storm pipe."

Actually, Pipe looked like he had been pulled from a tar pit. His long hair was dirty and knotted and tangled with dark mud.

"A terrier is somewhere in him," said the chief, smiling. "To find it, I'll need to give him a trim and a shampoo."

I guessed a storm pipe had crossed the stranger's path, too. He looked as wild and rumpled as the first day I had seen him. He hadn't shaved, and his shoes didn't have shoelaces. He was a lot older than my dad, who gives his age as "fortysomething." The chief's hair was gray, and his eyes had wrinkles. Still, I liked his face. It looked kid-friendly and sort of grandfatherly. It also looked tired, like he hadn't gotten much sleep.

"Are you one of the hurricane people?" I asked.

My mom would have had a fit if she had heard me being such a busybody, but that's the way I am. The stranger didn't seem to mind my question.

He smiled. "Yes, I am."

I had seen the pictures on the television of the flattened houses, flooding, and people without any place to go.

"There was nothing left to go back to," he added. "And I didn't like where they were putting us. Pipe and I don't take much to shelters, so we came here. We needed some space."

I glanced around the lot, wondering if he needed quite this much. But I didn't say so.

"How long are you staying?"

"I guess that depends on how soon they let me go back," he said.

That didn't sound very soon. Didn't he just say there was nothing to go back to?

I looked at the tent. He was right. It wasn't much to look at. It was the ugliest tepee I had ever seen. It had been put together with three different colors of old tarpaulins. Some crooked tree limbs held it up.

"You're going to live there?" I asked, pointing to the tent.

The chief nodded. "At least for a while. Me and Pipe."

It seemed a sorry state of affairs to have to live in an ugly tepee with a dirty dog named Pipe. It was bad enough living by himself.

"Where do you go to the bathroom?"

I could see my mom's hands trying to throttle me, but it was out. I just had to know. We dived for pop flies and kicked soccer balls in this lot.

The chief cackled loudly. Pipe's sleepy eyelids lifted in alarm. For a moment, the laugh worried me, too. I remembered what Irene had said about him being crazy. How funny can bathroom business be?

"I go to McDonald's," he explained. "The manager lets me use the restroom there."

McDonald's was a good option. It was just around the corner.

"But you're eating here, right?" I asked, pointing to the grill.

The chief nodded again and said, "Yes, outdoor cooking is much better for you."

This was news to me. We did it just for fun at our house, and that was mostly on the weekends. I would have to tell my dad.

"Well, mister, I better get going," I said.

I had learned about as much as I needed to. He had escaped from a hurricane and found a dog in a storm pipe. He slept in a tent, used the restroom at McDonald's, and cooked outside. There was probably more to know, but I didn't want to be a pest.

"Thanks for visiting," he said as I turned toward my bike.

"Thanks for cleaning our lot," I said.

"You're welcome."

"I don't own it," I clarified, so he wouldn't think I did. "My friends and I play here sometimes."

"It's a nice lot for playing," he agreed.

Then I rode my bike home.

I didn't tell anyone about my visit.

My mom would have said, "I don't want you going back there. Do you hear me?"

My dad would have said, "Listen to your mother."

Irene would have freaked out.

I kept Gooter on the sidelines, too. I knew that if I told him, he'd want to pay a visit. Then he'd want to start a game or just hang out. He'd exercise his territorial rights, and that didn't seem like a good idea, especially not with a man and his dog newly moved here from a hurricane and needing some space. So I didn't stir up anybody's anxiety.

On our way to church on Sunday, I noticed that the chief had Pipe sitting on the grill. I saw a pair of scissors in his hand, so I knew Pipe's tangled fur was about to come off. But no one else in our car had a clue.

"My God, he's eating dogs!" Irene screamed.

My dad suddenly did something he had never done before. He actually took his eyes off the road.

"Harold, should we call animal control?" my mom exclaimed.

Instantly, my dad sped up. He may have wanted to spare us the sight of blood.

I raised my voice and said, "That's his dog. He's just giving him a trim."

My dad continued to accelerate. My mom turned around to get a better view. Irene covered her eyes.

"I can't look!" she cried.

"Charlie, I think you're right," my mom agreed. "He's giving the little fellow a haircut. Look, Harold."

Our Plymouth slowed and then stopped. Everyone, except Irene, looked back.

"How do you know it's his dog?" she demanded.

"I see him from the bus every day, that's how," I said. "The dog lives there." You have to think fast when you have a hysterical sister.

"Poor man. I wonder how he's getting by," my mom asked.

I could have answered, "Outdoor cooking." I could have told them that it was better for you, too. But I kept my mouth shut. I hoped my dad would speed up again. I had never wanted to get to church so badly.

"I'm surprised he's still here," my dad said as we began to move. "The government is supposed to be helping those people."

"Maybe some of them don't like the shelters," I suggested.

The lot disappeared behind us.

Poor Pipe. Being trimmed atop an outdoor grill for everyone to see.

"I want all of us to say a prayer for him," my mom advised as we neared the church.

Under her breath, Irene muttered, "No way!"

In church, I began to wonder. That sometimes happens to me in church; between the preaching and the praying, I wonder. I wondered how the chief put milk on his cereal if he didn't have a refrigerator to keep it cold. I wondered what he used for silverware and plates. I wondered how he cooked in the rain. I wondered how he kept mosquitoes out of his tent. I wondered if he slept on the ground or an air mattress. I wondered about his clothes, too. After all, if he wore the same ones every day, when would he get a chance to wash them?

I wondered about his money. I wondered if he had enough to buy charcoal and dog food, but not enough for a new shirt and pants. I wondered if he had bought scissors to trim Pipe instead of razors to shave himself.

I wondered how he could feel safe at night. I wondered how he could sleep with the street lights on. I wondered how he did his "business" when McDonald's wasn't open.

Then I wondered about the future. I wondered what would happen when November came, the nights got cold, and the ground froze. I wondered what would become of his homemade tent when it snowed. I wondered what would happen to the chief if he caught pneumonia or got frostbite from sleeping outside.

Even for me, it was a lot of wondering.

Just before our service ended, when the reverend asked everybody to pray for those who were sick, those on their way to heaven, and those who had already gotten there, I offered one for Chief Goodyear down the street. Of course, I knew I could do more. Prayer and wonder were only warm-ups, and something else had to be done.

Monday morning at the bus stop, Gooter said, "Let's play ball after school."

I knew what that meant. He wanted to go the lot.

Instead of coming up with an excuse to not go, like my orthodontist appointment or helping my mom wash storm windows, I just played dumb.

"I don't know," I said.

I couldn't tell him that I'd already paid a visit to the lot.

"Afraid the chief is gonna scalp you, or what?" he dared.

Gooter always dared me and left little room to maneuver, unless I wanted to look like a kid who didn't believe in something impossible, like a stranger scalping two eleven-year-olds next to a hardware store. Of course, anything was possible.

"See you there," I said.

If I didn't go, he'd ask Stewart, Norman, or the Van Patten twins. Maybe he'd ask all of them, and that would make a crowd.

When I arrived that afternoon, Gooter was already there, tossing pop flies to himself. I noticed he was staying near the sidewalk.

"Hey, the squatter's got a dog," he whispered as soon as I pulled up. His voice made it sound like having a pet was some kind of conspiracy.

I tried to look surprised as I stared at the napping Pipe. With his fur trimmed, he was now a brown dog. The chief had revealed the terrier beneath the storm pipe. His short coat shined in the sunlight, like one of those canines in the dog food commercials.

"Maybe the guy is lonely," I suggested.

"Maybe he's staying," countered Gooter.

"Maybe," I said.

"Just so he knows that it's our lot."

The tent hadn't changed since my last visit. It was still the saddest-looking excuse for a tepee in our town. I wondered if the chief was stretched out inside, napping like before. If he came out and tried to recognize me, I was going to play it cool. I had my St. Louis Cardinals cap pulled down tight, giving my face plenty of shadow. In a Cardinals cap, one kid looked pretty much like another.

We edged onto the lot, tossing the ball. I felt kind of strange doing it, like I was playing in someone's backyard without permission. It felt like trespassing. But Gooter didn't seem to mind.

"He moved all of our stones," he complained, pointing to the pile.

"Trash, too," I said.

I threw him a ground ball that he lifted cleanly. Without

stones and trash, the fielding was easier.

"What do think is in those tires?" he asked, looking toward the stack with its cardboard cover and stone on top.

"Bathroom, maybe?" I dared.

Gooter stopped in the middle of a pitch. He made a face like he had swallowed a mouthful of sour milk. "Gross!"

"Want to check it out?"

"No way!"

Gooter immediately put distance between himself and the chief's tires, moving to the other end of the lot. As soon as we spread out, he started shouting for line drives and cussing when he missed one. I knew what he was doing. He wanted to be sure the chief heard us. He was being territorial. It was pure Gooter.

But the chief didn't show. I was beginning to wonder if he was there when Gooter threw a high one that I couldn't have caught with a step ladder. The ball hit the chief's grill and bounced hard off the tent. Pipe lifted his sleepy eyelids when it dropped near his feet.

"Nice one," I said.

"Sorry," Gooter called.

Both of us watched the tent, expecting action. I had seen it before, but no one stirred this time.

Gooter waited for me to fetch the ball, but I kneeled to tie my sneaker instead. Wild throws belonged to the thrower. That was our rule.

"What are you waiting for?" I said finally.

Gooter approached. His voice suddenly got quieter.

"You think he's in there?" he asked, pointing his glove at the tepee.

I shrugged. I could have said he was out scalping natives, but I resisted.

Gooter wandered to his left, trying to get a better angle on things.

"That tent shouldn't be here anyway," he protested, still whispering.

"Get the ball," I said.

Gooter punched his glove and headed for the tent. But he only got as far as the grill.

Pipe jumped up and revved his chainsaw motor. "Not so fast," he seemed to growl.

I watched Gooter freeze. He turned to look at me.

"What do I do now?" he asked.

"Stay away from the grill," I advised.

He backed up, raising his hands as if Pipe had a gun. He circled wide, trying to sneak up on the tent from behind. But Pipe had him on radar now. As Gooter circled, the little dog followed in an arc, stretching on his leash.

"He won't bite," I said, though I wasn't entirely sure of this. Pipe didn't look mean. Like Gooter, he was just territorial.

Obviously, the chief wasn't in his tent. Not even a homeless person could sleep through the ruckus Pipe was making. I wondered if he had gone to McDonald's.

I was relieved not to see him. It's better to not find someone home if the only business you have visiting is to make him feel like he shouldn't be at home. I didn't know if Gooter would say something I would regret.

For the moment, he was busy getting our ball back while Pipe was furious with him for daring to try. The little dog pulled at his stake, following Gooter's every move and snapping at him. I couldn't help but admire the effort. It made me wonder if a storm pipe had anything to do with it. When Gooter found a stick and tried to roll the ball clear of the tent, Pipe grabbed that, too. He just wore Gooter out.

"Ah, let 'em keep it," he said finally, walking away disgusted. "I'm tired of this place!"

I was glad to hear Gooter say it.

That week, my mom took Irene and me to McDonald's for dinner. She does that when my dad is out of town. You may not believe this, but my dad has never stepped inside a McDonald's. He hasn't even gone in there to use the restroom. It's become one of his resolutions in life to never cross the Golden Arches. My mom says his tombstone will read:

Harold Roebecker
Devoted Husband, Loving Father
Never Set Foot in McDonald's

I, on the other hand, go there at least once a week. This time when I entered, I scanned for the chief on one of his trips to the restrooms. McDonald's can sometimes be a small world.

Then I spotted him. But it wasn't where I expected. Wearing a McDonald's uniform, he was behind the counter at the french fry station, sprinkling salt on a field of fries.

My jaw dropped at the sight. It was definitely him, but he looked different. A hat covered his wild hair. His face seemed thinner, too. Then I realized why. The chief had shaved. He had shaved and come to work at McDonald's!

I eased behind my mom, staying out of view.

What if he recognized me? What if he said, "Hey there! How you doing?" What if my mom asked, "Charlie, do you know that man?" What if Irene screamed, "He's the one who eats dogs!"

This wasn't the time for introductions, so I told my mom to order me a burger and a Coke.

"No fries, dear?" she asked loudly.

I shook my head. No fries. "I'll get us a seat," I said, and then quickly disappeared into a corner booth. It was the best spot to keep out of sight until the food arrived. It was also the best place for spying. From there, I watched the chief salt and bag fries. Then I watched him go to the soft drink dispenser and push some buttons. For a new guy, he knew the terrain.

Had he worked at McDonald's before the hurricane?

When my mom came with our tray, Irene insisted we move to a window booth. She was just being contrary. As we ate, I watched her pop fries into her mouth.

If she only knew who bagged them.

With a uniform to wear, the chief would finally have a chance to wash his clothes. Maybe he had them soaking somewhere right now. And he could bring leftovers home for Pipe. Working at McDonald's had its upside.

Then Irene said, "Charlie, get me some ketchup, would ya?"

"Why don't you get it yourself?" I replied. Obviously, I didn't want to get spotted. Besides, she had two legs.

My mom made her "you'd better be nice to your sister" face, so I got up and angled my way toward the dispensers, counting on the crowd for cover.

Please let me be just one more kid in the madhouse.

Just as I got to the counter and was about to reach for the ketchup cups, a familiar voice caught me like a hook.

"Hey there! How you doing?"

The chief was replenishing the napkins and straws.

"Hi, mister," I said, trying to look surprised. The madhouse hadn't saved me. "Are you working here?"

He smiled and said, "Started a few days ago. They were hiring, and I was coming here anyway."

This wasn't the time for a chat. He was working, and I was trying to get out of there.

"Well, my sister needs ketchup," I said urgently, as if

Irene might go into a coma without it. "See ya."

I pumped some ketchup into a cup and ran back to the booth.

When I got there, Irene said, "What took you so long?"

She was being her usual disagreeable self. Neither she nor my mom had observed me. Still, I wasn't about to risk another close encounter with the chief, so I retreated to the restroom, where I washed my hands more times than I needed to. I calculated how long my mom and Irene would take to finish their food, then I ran for the exit.

On the way home, I pondered the strange turn of events. The chief was working in a place where my dad had sworn that he would never enter. So now there were two men on the planet who would never cross paths in McDonald's.

With the chief at work, I could only watch for Pipe from the bus. The little dog looked lonesome.

On Saturday, I biked to Hildreth's again, but I didn't want glue or kite string this time. I wanted to visit Pipe.

I first went to McDonald's to make sure that the chief was okay with my visit. It was funny how things change. The week before, I had considered him to be the intruder. Now I was the one asking for permission.

The chief was wiping tabletops near the windows.

"Hey there, kiddo," he said.

I noticed a nametag on his shirt.

"I don't even know your name," he said.

"Charlie," I replied.

The chief pointed to his nametag and said, "You can call me Bill."

Bill? Just plain Bill?

I liked Chief Goodyear better. In my house, kids didn't call adults by their first names.

"Weren't you just in here last night, Charlie?"

I nodded. He gave me a sly look.

"It's not good to eat too much fast food," he said.

"I know," I answered. I hadn't seen the movie *Super Size Me*, but I'd heard about it. It was the story of some guy who lived on McDonald's food for a month and nearly died.

"Balance is everything," said the chief. "I see many of the same faces in here every day. Families, too."

I listened, thinking he didn't have to worry about my family.

"Is it all right if I visit Pipe?" I asked.

Bill bent down to pick up the flattened remains of what looked like an Egg McMuffin.

"Sure, go ahead," he answered cheerily. "He'll be glad for the company. I've had to leave him by himself these days, but one of us has to work. I don't want the little fellow to starve."

I should have thought about these words, but my mind was already operating in that faraway place where a kid goes when he's thinking about a dog.

"Does Pipe like chicken nuggets?"

Bill smiled and said, "I would dare say that he loves them."

"Then I'll take him some."

"That's very kind of you, Charlie," he replied.

As I dug out quarters from my pockets, I decided to ask something that wasn't really my business.

"Did you work at McDonald's before you came here? You know the job really well."

He shook his head and said, "No, Charlie, I worked for a landscaper before the storm. I'm an arborist."

"What's that?" I asked.

"I take care of trees," he replied. "I plant them, prune them, and make sure they grow straight and stay healthy. I give them a better chance to live. Of course, where I come from, there aren't a lot of trees left standing now. Not a lot of anything standing."

I nodded. Being an arborist in hurricane country sounded like a risky way to make a living.

"You like working here?"

Bill stopped to wipe another table. "Oh, yes," he said. "It's a good meanwhile job."

"Meanwhile?"

"While I'm waiting."

"To go back? Right?"

"Yes. To go home."

My mom had taught me that no one likes a spoilsport, especially one with cable television. So I kept my mouth shut about the news reports that I had seen. They were saying that the hurricane people wouldn't be going home for months. I counted my quarters instead.

"Well, I better buy the nuggets," I said.

"Yes, of course," replied the chief. "Thanks for thinking of us, Charlie."

"Sure," I said, wondering what he meant by "us."

I moved to the counter, where I plopped down $2.99 without even looking at the menu. I knew the price of chicken nuggets by heart.

At the lot, Pipe fired up his chainsaw growl as soon as I approached the tent. What was left of Gooter's baseball—a chewed cover and some tangled twine—was under his feet.

I opened the box of nuggets, letting the smell of warm chicken hit him. The first whiff shut him up. He wagged his tail and then sat at attention like he was a dog at a state dinner. Suddenly, Pipe was the politest dog on the planet.

I sat on the ground beside the tent, and Pipe sat on my lap. We renewed our acquaintance over nuggets, then over the empty box of nuggets, and, finally, over my greasy, nugget-smelling fingers.

Then I peeked into Bill's tepee. Some people might have considered it snooping, but I was sitting near the entrance anyway. Inside, it looked pitiful.

When my dad and I went camping, we filled our tent with so much stuff there was hardly any room left for us. Air mattresses. Sleeping bags. Cookware. Canteens. Lanterns. Flashlights. A battery-operated television. Board games. A deck of cards. We also brought enough food to feed a platoon.

Inside Bill's homemade tepee was a lot of bare ground, a thin strip of carpet, a solitary pot, and a stack of canned goods. I recognized tuna fish and Campbell's soup. Sardines were there, too.

The sight drove a cold stake right through me, and it wasn't just because I hated sardines. I guess I had expected more. I didn't think there would be so much bare ground. Bill was practically camped in a cave.

I stood and shook myself, still feeling that coldness inside me. My dad had said something about the government helping these people. My mom had asked us to pray. Meanwhile, an arborist without trees was working at McDonald's and living in a cave tent with canned goods and a dog he had saved from a storm pipe.

Finally, I knew what had to be done.

II

WHEN WE ARRIVED HOME with our Christmas trees, Irene made good on her promise to quarantine my puny pine.

"Do not bring that thing into this house," she said as our dad manhandled the big tree off the car roof and headed toward our front door.

"Mind your own business," I replied.

"The garage is the only place for it," she added. "At least we won't have to look at it there."

I had planned to take it to the garage anyway so I could fix it up, but I couldn't say that now.

"I'm going to put it on the front lawn with lights and tinsel so the whole neighborhood can see it."

"No, you won't."

"Will, too."

"Will not."

"Children," said my mom. She had come outside to watch our dad struggle with the tree. "Please, no bickering. It's almost Christmas."

"Will, too," I whispered when Irene followed my mom inside.

I generally never gave Irene the last word … not even at Christmas.

The garage was out of the question now. Putting it there would have looked like surrender, so I stood my tree on the porch instead. Then I stepped back to examine it.

Standing by itself without its piney brothers towering above it like giant sequoias, the puny tree didn't look so small anymore. In fact, it looked about the right size. Naturally, its defects remained. It was still scrawny. Its trunk was crooked, the branches lopsided, and its top hadn't made it down from Canada or wherever it had been chopped off. The orange sap and white wounds hadn't disappeared either. Still, it was perfect. The possibility was definitely there for a tree miracle.

I stood on the porch admiring it until I heard the call to come into the house. Inside, everyone was staring at Irene's perfect tree in our living room. My dad had set it up on its stand. The top almost touched the ceiling.

"What a lovely tree, Harold," bubbled my mom.

"Irene picked it out," he confessed. "She has an eye for trees."

Irene beamed like she had gotten a medal. Then she gave me her secret smirk. There was no way that I was going to let that pass.

"It looks cloned to me," I said.

The family stopped staring.

"What do you mean, Charlie?" my dad asked. Something in his voice wanted to know how I knew about cloning.

"It doesn't look real. It looks like it came out of a tree mold."

"Oh," he replied. "Yes ... well ... it does have a very traditional shape."

"You're just jealous," snapped Irene. "Because yours is so ugly."

My mom gave my dad a puzzled look.

"Charlie got a tree, too," he explained. "A small one."

"A sick, midget tree," added Irene. "It got puked from the forest."

"That's enough," my mom said.

"Irene's tree took steroids," I shot back. "It looks like the Arnold Schwarzenegger of Christmas trees."

"Dad!"

Our dad raised both hands and said, "Okay, you two, get ready for supper. And no more discussion of trees. Each of you got the one you wanted, so both of you should be happy."

As Irene retreated to the kitchen, she said, "At least my tree is in the house."

I had a comeback ready, but I stopped myself. What I wanted to say couldn't be said without tipping my hand.

Sure, her tree was in the house, and mine wasn't. Sure, her tree stood tall, and my tree looked puny. Sure, her tree was full, and my tree was scrawny. But, like so many others, her tree was standing in a living room while mine was going somewhere special. But I couldn't say it.

For the first time, I let Irene have the last word.

A long time ago, Irene was actually normal. She was even nice. Not sweet; I don't overdo my adjectives. I'll just say that she was nice, maybe even normal nice. She used to laugh every time I did something stupid. She knew my name, too. Sometimes she even gave me compliments like, "Awesome look, Charlie," when I wore my Hawaiian shirt on the day I had to give an oral report at school.

Nowadays, she doesn't call me Charlie. ("Is *he* coming too?") Instead of compliments, I get complaints and threats. ("Better not, or I'll tell mom.") When I'm not invisible, I'm just a "bug-eyed creep."

She used to be fun. On car trips, she read Shel Silverstein, and we'd laugh together at the crazy pictures. She was even funny sometimes. She did a hilarious impersonation of my Aunt Marion. It made me laugh so hard that I cried. When I ask her to do it now, she tells me to get lost.

She used to be generous, too. She gave me her leftover fries at McDonald's. She shared her Halloween loot. She let me listen to her music. She loaned me her CD player for Boy Scout trips. She even participated in a five-kilometer run for these boys in Sudan. She didn't even know the boys, but she ran for them.

Now she wears a T-shirt that sums up her stinginess. It says, "It's all about me!" She wears it at least twice a week. I sometimes think she does it just to bother me.

My mom told me that it was only a phase. She said that I'd go through it, too, but I don't think so. I could never be that stingy. Even Gooter, who is territorial and a poor loser, will give away half his lunch if yours falls out of a locker or ends up at the bottom of a stampede at recess. Compared to Irene, Gooter is Mother Teresa.

So how could I expect her to understand that a homeless man needed a Christmas tree, even if it was a puny Christmas tree without a top? How could I expect her to be nice? Being generous and nice had belonged to the other Irene, the one before the shirt. Living with the sister I had now was like living with a stranger.

When I left Bill's tent that Saturday morning in October, I knew exactly where I was headed. I went straight to the bottom shelf of my mom's linen closet, where she stored our bedding.

The sight of that thin carpet stretched on the bare ground kept replaying in my head like a bad music video. First I saw the chief lying on it, tossing and turning. Then I saw him lying under it, tossing and turning. Next I saw him trying to roll up in it.

I couldn't imagine anyone sleeping on the ground

without a blanket or a pillow, so I grabbed one of each from the linen closet. I borrowed a pillowcase, too. Then I snagged two facecloths and a couple hand towels. We had plenty of both.

Remaining out of sight in the garage, I tied everything onto my bike rack. Then a better idea came to me. I'd let the chief have my mummy bag. With cold nights coming, he needed it more than I did. Besides, my parents had promised me a new one for my birthday.

I spotted my dad's foam ground pad, the one that had touched the soil of seven continents (Antarctica might have been a stretch) when he was younger. All that traveling had worn out both of them. The pad had patches, and my dad didn't hop continents anymore. He wouldn't mind giving it to a good cause. The point was to get Bill off the ground.

Fortunately, Saturday mornings at our house were ideal for prowling in the closets. Irene slept until noon. Even then, she begged for overtime. My mom always did the grocery shopping, and my dad went to his Army Reserve meetings twice a month.

Still, eyes were watching outside. Mrs. Simon, our nosy widow neighbor, always had her face in the window. Mr. Hatch was our chatty mailman. He usually appeared precisely at the wrong moment. Once, he even caught me answering nature's urgent call behind the oleanders. Either of these two might phone my mom to ask why I was exiting the house with a pillow, towels, and a sleeping bag tied to my BMX bike. Was I running away from home? So I pedaled like crazy once I left the garage.

When I got to the lot, I did a quick ride-by to make sure the chief wasn't back from McDonald's. Then I parked my bike next to the tepee. Pipe didn't growl. Instead he wagged his tail and searched for chicken nuggets. He sniffed everything, but he only picked up the scents of laundry soap, musty garage, and the soil of seven continents. As usual, the area around the tent was swept. The chief sure kept a clean camp.

I piled everything inside the tent, but I made sure it was out of Pipe's reach. Then I biked home. I didn't want any of our lot gang to see me, especially Gooter. I also didn't want the chief to know who had been there. Some people don't take charity well. They don't see it for what it really is: the chance to give away something you don't need anymore.

The following week, we visited my grandmother in Huntsville. The next weekend, my mom took Irene and me to shop for winter coats at the factory outlets in Jefferson. Shopping just about killed my patience.

When I finally got a free Saturday, I gathered a few more essentials for the chief, including a flashlight with batteries and a saucepan my mom had put in the box for the Salvation Army. I added a few pieces of silverware, too. Because it was still a mystery what the chief used for dishes, I threw in a mug, a dinner plate, and a soup bowl. All were taken from the deepest corners of our kitchen cupboards.

I packed everything in a large pail, which I was also going to donate. Every campsite needs a pail for water, laundry, washing dishes, or just sitting around. It had to be more comfortable than tires.

Pretending not to remember me, Pipe started growling when I got there. Then I unwrapped a stuffed pork chop that I pulled from refrigerated leftovers. That cured his amnesia.

I felt better when I looked in the tent this time. The stuff left from my first trip had found a home. The sleeping bag was stretched across my dad's foam ground pad. The pillow was tucked in the opening. My mom's towels were folded neatly. The thin strip of carpet had become Pipe's new bed.

I waited another week before I visited McDonald's. The chief was busy on the drive-thru lane when I arrived, so I rode my bike around to the window.

"Hey, Charlie," he said, looking surprised. "I think this is supposed to be for cars."

"It's okay," I replied. "The sign doesn't say so. I just wanted to know if I can visit Pipe again."

"Sure, you can walk him if you want. I didn't have a chance this morning."

"*No problema,*" I answered, practicing my Spanish vocabulary like Señora Burns, my teacher, had told me.

"A walk around the lot will be fine. Just keep him on his leash. Okay?"

"*Bueno.*"

"Don't worry about his little deposits. I'll pick those up."

"Sounds fair," I said, switching back to English. On the topic of deposits, I wanted to be sure nothing was lost in translation.

Bill smiled, but his face soon turned quizzical.

"I've been wanting to ask. Have you seen anyone visiting my tent?"

I was ready for it, so I said, "Just me when I went to see Pipe."

That was the carefully worded truth. I tried to look interested, but not too much.

Bill nodded and said, "Someone's been leaving me things like towels and dishes. Even a sleeping bag. I thought you might know something about it."

He was looking at me with the X-ray stare that adults use when they want to read the truth behind your eyes. Another kid might have blinked. Not me.

"A lot of charitable people live in this town," I offered. "It would be hard to pick one. When that tsunami hit last year, our church filled a whole semi with stuff to send. A lot of sleeping bags were in it." I stopped because you never want to say too much about charity.

Bill nodded gravely. "Yes, I know. I gave some blankets, too. It was terrible."

He was still looking at me, but the X-ray gaze was gone. I was impenetrable. I guess tsunamis have a way of detouring an investigation.

Cars were backing up in the drive-thru lane. I watched the chief shift gears and go back to work.

"What will it be, Charlie? Nuggets again?"

"Nothing," I said. "I'm taking your advice about not eating so much fast food."

"Oh."

"I just wanted to check about going to see Pipe. That's all."

"Thank you, Charlie."

His McDonald's voice had returned. It was time for me to pull ahead.

"*Adios.*"

At the lot, I walked Pipe on his leash. He was like one of those dogs in prison camp movies, patrolling the perimeter. But those dogs don't ever seem to mark the walls or leave deposits. I guess Pipe would never go to Hollywood.

I was tying him back to his stake when a voice called out from the sidewalk.

"Roebecker, you dog thief!"

When I looked up, I saw Gooter jumping off his bike.

I tried not to look like it was a big deal. Gooter and I are best buddies because we have a lot in common. We have snooty sisters and trouble with fractions. We don't like green vegetables. And we show up where we're not supposed to be. I used to wonder if we were brothers in a previous life. Gooter said it's because we live in a small town where boys looking for the extraordinary are naturally going to run into each other. In our town, there definitely isn't a whole lot of extraordinary.

I took my time making sure that I tied Pipe's leash tight. I secretly hoped he would remember Gooter from his last visit and fire up some fury.

Pipe locked on him, growled for a second, and then gave a welcoming wag of his tail as if Gooter was an old friend. I stared, not quite believing it.

"That stupid dog owes us a ball," Gooter said.

"I think he ate it," I replied. The cover and twine weren't around.

"What are you tying him up for?"

"So he won't run away."

"Let him run away. Then we can play."

I couldn't tell if Gooter was kidding or not. He sometimes took a joke to the edge.

"Can't. It's not our dog."

Gooter looked around the lot. "Are you snooping or something?" he asked.

"Sort of. I went to McDonald's and then rode by." Both true.

"Every time I come, the guy is never around," said Gooter.

I didn't offer any explanations. Obviously, he didn't know that the chief was working at McDonald's.

"What are *you* doing?" I asked. I wanted him to know that I wasn't the only one without any business in the neighborhood.

Gooter shrugged and said, "Just keeping an eye on things. Hey, it's still our lot."

Gooter was being territorial again. He moved to the tepee entrance, bending to look inside.

"Man, he's got dishes and stuff in here. Look!"

I knew I shouldn't. It wasn't the same as dropping off charity. But I stuck my head in anyway. I tried to seem curious, but I hoped no one would see us. I also didn't want Gooter recognizing my mummy bag from Sean Miller's sleepover the year before.

"Looks pretty poor to me," I said, backing out.

"Yeah. Like in Africa."

Gooter was always connecting to Africa. It was probably because he watched so much National Geographic.

"I bet it's no fun living here," I remarked.

"My dad says he's from the hurricane."

"I heard that, too," I said. I could have added that I heard it from the chief himself, but I was watching my words.

Gooter studied the grill.

"I want to feel sorry for him," he said. "It's a bad deal getting run off by a hurricane, but I just wish he'd picked another place to camp."

"I guess some people need space," I said. "Mr. Hildreth hasn't made him leave."

"Yeah, but Fuzzy Jergon just got a new soccer goal for his birthday. The folding, portable kind. He was going to bring it to the lot. When I told him about losing our ball, he said his dad would kill him if something happened to the net."

"Maybe we'll have to pick another place to play," I said.

"Until he leaves."

"How much longer is that going to be? It's almost Halloween."

"Halloween doesn't have anything to do with it. I bet he's just waiting to go home. Waiting for the water to go down or whatever."

Gooter seemed to consider this.

I added, "The best thing we can do is be Christian about it. Imagine having all your stuff underwater. It must be awful. At least he has dry ground here."

"I suppose," Gooter agreed. His voice sounded less territorial than usual. Then he pointed at the stack of tires and said, "But he could go to the bathroom someplace else. That's gross."

I said, "It's not his bathroom, Gooter. I checked it out. Come on."

I headed toward the tires, but he hung back. When I removed the stone and cardboard and stuck my hand in the hole to lift the bag of charcoal, Gooter's eyes bugged out as if he had bitten into a jalapeño straight out of the can. Then he saw the bag.

"Dude!" he cried. He ran to see for himself.

"That is so not cool," he said, sounding relieved.

I couldn't tell him everything I knew, but I could tell him what was most important.

"The chief's not messing with our lot, Gooter. He's just trying to get by."

Gooter stared at the contents of the tire hole.

"Yeah," he said. "I see what you mean."

At school, they gave us donation boxes to carry around with our trick-or-treat bags on Halloween so people could give money for the hurricane victims. It seemed like a good idea. That night, trick-or-treating on our street, I filled my box. A lot of generous people live in the neighborhood. The next morning at the breakfast table, as I stared at the words "Hurricane Victims" on the donation box, I got another idea.

Why shouldn't I give this donation to the chief, our very own hurricane victim, and save the trouble of sending it off?

I could add in Gooter's box and a couple others. I even

considered delivering them myself. When I mentioned my idea to Gooter, he didn't like it.

"That's stealing, Charlie," he said.

"No it's not," I replied. "The money is for the victims. We're just delivering it."

"We're only supposed to collect it," he said. "Besides, the boxes are numbered. We have to return them empty or full."

He was right. But did a donation box have to be only empty or only full?

"How about if we take half the money out, give it to the chief, then turn the other half in?" I might not be good at fractions, but I still knew the basics.

Gooter stared a me like I was crazy. "Dude, do you want to go to jail?"

That scared me because Gooter doesn't usually use jail as an excuse not to do something. So that was the end of it. I turned in my box, and he did, too.

In November, people started raking leaves and wearing coats. Kids on the bus didn't pay attention to Hildreth's lot anymore. The chief's campsite became something ordinary on our route, like pumpkins on doorsteps. Our soccer games relocated to Fuzzy Jergon's backyard, and Gooter stopped his territorial talk of taking over the lot.

On our drive to church every Sunday, I always turned to

see if the chief was on the lot. Naturally, Irene never wasted an opportunity to voice her opinion.

"I don't understand why you keep looking at that horrible place," she'd say.

For the next two weekends, my dad kept me busy around the house with yard work. I had to rake and bag leaves. Then I had to carry the bags and empty them. Even Irene had to help, which was some consolation because she hates leaves.

Though I didn't have a chance to visit the lot or McDonald's, I still prowled our closets looking for stuff to take to the chief. I also inspected the Salvation Army box more thoroughly. I found some great stuff. The teakettle without a cover would still work for boiling water. There was my dad's cardigan pullover that he never wore. Blue elephants on beige weren't really him. The gardening gloves weren't lined, but they still might keep the chief's hands warm. He could use the handheld mirror for shaving. There was also a really old thermos, a knit ski hat from when my parents lived in Vermont, and a pocket sewing kit with four different-colored threads. I also found the bedpan from when my grandfather had lived with us and couldn't climb stairs. I let it stay. Even charity has its limits.

When I was done, my backpack was nearly full. I even made room for a pair of men's woolen socks that I found in a box marked "church rummage sale" and two cans of Hormel Chili.

I didn't have a chance to deliver anything until Veteran's Day. With school out, my dad in the parade, and my mom on the VFW refreshment committee, it was the perfect chance to escape. But Bill was home when I arrived.

I started to ride past the lot, but he saw me.

"Hey, Charlie," he called out.

I waved as if I was in a hurry to go somewhere else, but his invite tested my good manners.

"Come over and say hi to Pipe."

I left my bike at the curb and dropped the backpack to the ground.

At the tent, Pipe immediately sniffed me over. In return, I gave him a rowdy face-cuddle.

"Pipe is getting spoiled," said the chief, chuckling. "Chicken nuggets *and* canned cat food. Can you believe it? That charitable person left four cans. Pipe likes them so much that he doesn't want to eat dry dog food anymore."

I tried to chuckle too, but I'm not a good at it. I hadn't brought any cat food to the tent.

"I sure would like to know who this person is," the chief mused, giving me another of those X-ray looks.

I noticed a shopping bag behind Pipe. I wanted to move the conversation along, so I asked, "Been to the mall?"

Shaking his head, he said, "No, the charitable soul left that, too. Two brand-new pairs of socks. Still in the package. I found it when I got back."

If I was on the chief's list of suspects, the surprise on my face instantly cleared me of suspicion. And I wasn't faking.

"New stuff, huh?" I said, glancing at the sidewalk where my backpack remained with those socks for the rummage sale inside.

So I wasn't the only one on a charitable mission?

"You were right about the generous people in this town, Charlie. I guess someone must think I'm staying for the winter."

My mind darted through a briar patch of possibilities. A charitable mom? Someone on the bus? Gooter?

Gooter's dad owned a clothing store, but Gooter didn't have a cat. It was probably someone I didn't know.

"Whoever it is, I sure do appreciate it," continued the chief. "But I hope to be out of here by Christmas."

I started listening again.

"Going back home?"

"Not that soon. They're still pumping water from where I lived. No one is going to be let back for months."

If he was keeping up on current events, there wasn't really a point for me to hold back on the grim outlook.

"On the TV, they're saying it's going to be years," I agreed.

"I'm going to Florida," said the chief. "It's warmer there."

"Florida?"

I wanted to say that hurricanes liked warm weather, too, but I figured he knew that.

"I might have a better chance there of finding the kind of work I do," he added.

I nodded. "Being an arborist, right?"

"Yes, you remembered."

"It's not an easy word to forget," I replied.

"No, it's not," he agreed.

"I like trees, too," I added. I did. I just didn't like raking their leaves.

Smiling, the chief said, "I'm glad to hear it, Charlie. Trees can teach us a lot about surviving and getting through the hard times. They are a lot tougher than most of us think. We can learn a lot from them."

This was news to me. I just liked the way they looked and the sound their leaves made in the wind. The shade could be a relief, too.

"I hope you find that kind of job," I said. Trees in Florida would be lucky to have the chief in their state.

"Thank you, Charlie. Me, too. But I first have to save a little more before I fold camp. It's two of us traveling now."

I looked at Pipe and I thought, "You're one lucky dog. This man is going to take care of you like a tree!"

That was the end of our conversation. I had to catch the end of the parade, and he had to work the lunch shift.

I said, "See ya!"

The chief walked me to the edge of the lot and watched me put on my backpack. Naturally, I wanted to make a quick getaway.

"What do you have in there?" he asked, pointing to the pack with its load of undelivered items.

I couldn't say books because it wasn't a school day.

"Just stuff," I answered, trying to sound like a kid without a vocabulary.

"I was reading about a study the other day," continued the chief. "It said kids are putting too many books in their packs. It's not good for you."

I nodded. He had said the same thing about fast food.

"I'll lighten it up," I said, riding off on my bike.

And I did. The next week, I lightened it up inside Bill's tent with everything from home. My sole witness was Pipe—the only dog on the planet who was as lucky as a tree.

As Thanksgiving neared, I found myself flirting with the idea of inviting the chief to our house for turkey dinner. The more I thought about it, the more it seemed to be a tricky proposition. I'd have to go public with our acquaintance and those trips to the lot. My parents would have to agree to the invite. I could hear Irene shrieking, "Invite who?" Finally, the chief would have to accept.

When I imagined what his Thanksgiving would be like on the lot, I pictured him sitting on his pail, eating a Big

Mac or a warmed-up can of chili while our family feasted on turkey with all the fixings. It didn't seem right. That cold stake started to stir in me again.

One evening at dinner, I tested the waters. My mom mentioned that my Uncle Will, Aunt Marion, and their kids might drive from Rockdale for the holiday.

"If people don't have a family, what do they for Thanksgiving?" I wondered aloud.

"People without family often go somewhere," replied my mom smoothly.

"Like a restaurant?" I ventured.

"Or friends invite them to dinner. Some may cook at home, too."

She had used the right word, the "home" word.

"And the homeless? They don't have a place to cook. What about them?"

My dad asked for the potatoes and then fielded my question.

"There are places that serve dinners, son. Rescue missions. Community soup kitchens."

I had heard of these places. "Like bread lines?" I asked.

Their forks stopped moving.

"Not exactly," said my mom. "People actually sit down to eat, dear. They get a complete meal."

"Where did you hear about bread lines?" my father asked, eyeing me over the bowl of potatoes.

"In social studies. We've been reading about the Great Depression."

They nodded and then began eating again. I was tempted to add that some folks were caught in a depression just as great today, but I left that to history.

My mom said, "This year, the ladies at the Safe Harbor Hospitality House are sponsoring a Thanksgiving lunch for the needy at the Crossroads Shelter. I'll be baking some pies."

That didn't sound bad … if they got pie.

"What about inviting someone to your house?" I asked.

I got puzzled looks from my parents.

"What do you mean?" inquired my dad while he served himself broccoli.

"Inviting a homeless person for Thanksgiving dinner. Do people do that?"

"No way! Don't even go there, mister!" cried Irene. "I don't want any stranger coming into our house. He could kill the whole family."

My dad swallowed swiftly and said, "Irene, those kinds of comments aren't necessary. I think you're watching too many movies."

It warmed my heart to hear it. I gave her my "Dad sure got you" smile.

"I bet you want to invite that creepy guy from the tent, don't you?" Irene said.

Sometimes, mostly by accident, Irene got it right. She

was dangerous in that way.

"What creepy guy?" I offered innocently, not missing a forkful of meatloaf.

I had to stay cool.

"You know who I mean. That man at Hildreth's. You're always looking at him when we drive by there. I've seen you on the bus."

"I've seen you staring at Billy Wetmore on the bus," I countered, "but I'm not making a big deal out of it."

"Billy Wetmore? What do you mean?" she said, trying to sound innocent. But her face revealed the truth. "I look at a lot of people. So?"

"Same here," I said. "But I don't ogle them."

Such a sorry sight just had to be reported.

"That's enough," said my dad, using his army voice. "Everyone eat."

Only the clicking of forks and the slurping of milk filled the silence that followed.

"As a rule, we don't invite people we don't know into our home, Charlie," advised my mom quietly. "It just isn't done ... unless there is an emergency or something like that."

Emergency? A homeless arborist working at McDonald's and living in a homemade tent with winter coming. Wasn't that an emergency?

For a moment, I debated if I should tell them everything. Then I decided against it. I had tested the family waters, and they were cold and unwelcoming. Besides, I couldn't let Irene know she had guessed right about my stares from the bus window. I would never have the last word again in our lifetimes.

The chief would have to settle for Thanksgiving sponsored by the Safe Harbor Hospitality House at the Crossroads Shelter.

Still, I dared a last stab at particulars.

"If homeless people don't have phones or mailboxes, how do they hear about the free turkey and pie?"

My mom smiled. She wore the same smile when she was standing in the Women's Auxiliary booth serving coffee cake for the hospital benefit.

"We publicize, dear. We put it in the paper and on the radio. We put up posters, and we give signs to the merchants."

"Like McDonald's?"

My mom frowned. "No, I don't think so. Fast-food chains have rules about local advertising. Don't they, Harold?"

"Don't ask me about McDonald's," my dad replied. "It's an alien planet as far as I'm concerned."

"I'm sure you'll see a sign at school," my mom said.

And she was right. The next week, a sign announcing the Thanksgiving lunch at the Crossroads Shelter was tacked to the community service bulletin board next to the gym lockers at school. When no one was looking, I took it down and stuffed it in my backpack. I delivered it to the chief's tent the afternoon before Thanksgiving. I also dropped off a bag of mixed nuts. We had two, but when my uncle and aunt canceled on us, I figured we could manage fine with one. And just in case the complete lunch my mom had raved about was missing the most important side dish of Pilgrim gratitude, I also left the chief a can of cranberry sauce.

I set the nuts and sauce next to his brand-new socks that were still in their package. So he wouldn't miss it, I placed the sign announcing the lunch on his sleeping bag. I never knew if he went.

Those first weeks in December, I supplied the chief with soap, Band-Aids, toothpaste, and toilet paper. Also Advil and Alka-Seltzer. We had plenty of both at our house.

I left pretzels, power bars, bottled water, and the most recent issues of *Time* magazine. My dad never read them anyway. I brought candles, matches, and extra batteries for the flashlight. I delivered packets of cocoa, envelopes of instant oatmeal, and a box of teabags. I hoped the food would help him stay warm. I even dropped off some vitamins and a calendar from our insurance agent.

I kept an eye open for that other charitable person, but I never saw anyone. That was a relief. Charity is better if it's anonymous, anyway.

I still wondered if it might be Gooter, so one day on the bus, without any warm-up to the subject, I asked, "Have you been by the lot?"

Gooter shook his head. "My dad has me working at the store unpacking clothes for the Christmas rush."

"Socks?" I asked, watching his face.

"Yeah, socks," he answered wearily. "About a zillion. Why?"

"Just wondering," I said. "In case I need a pair."

He didn't give away anything except the fact that he was tired of packaged clothing. It was hard to say if he was playing dumb.

By the fifteenth, it got chilly. As I ran to catch the bus one morning, our front lawn crunched under my feet. The brown grass was stiff with frost. I thought of the chief lying inside his sleeping bag with only a foam pad between him and the cold earth. I wondered if he would finally leave for Florida.

On the day that school let out for the holidays, I went straight to McDonald's. I needed to know if he was staying for Christmas.

To my surprise, I saw him sipping coffee at a table when I arrived. Christmas decorations hung on the window behind him, and holiday music played from the speakers. The chief only needed a newspaper to look like a regular customer.

When he saw me with an Oreo McFlurry, he waved at me and said, "Hey, Charlie. Sit down. You caught me on break."

For a moment, I thought he had quit and was hanging around for his pay. I sat down and sucked hard on my straw.

"If you've come to see Pipe, I'm afraid you won't find him home," he said. "I've put him in a shelter."

"A shelter?" I repeated, suddenly getting a brain freeze. It was part shock, part ice cream.

The chief lifted a finger and said, "Don't worry. He's fine. With the cool weather, I decided he would be better off under a roof, so I boarded him at the humane society. Don't you think it would be cruel to leave him outside this time of year?"

Actually, I hadn't thought about it. As soon as I did, I knew he was right. The same thing could be said about people sleeping outside, too.

"Yeah, we got frost at our house on Thursday," I said.

"It has been nippy in the mornings," he agreed. "When I feel cold, I get some coffee." He lifted his cup to show me. "But Pipe has to depend on others for help." He shook his head. "Let me tell you. It's tough having to depend on others."

I knew he was right. As a kid, I was the definition of dependent. It wasn't easy.

But I also had heard, mostly in church, that depending was part of living together. And I'm not just talking dogs and people.

"Poor fellow," mused the chief. "I miss him already. He

didn't like the move. New scenery. New company. New smells. He had to have his shots so he could stay. He was not a happy camper when I left him, but neither of us is much for shelters."

"Is that because they're crowded and smelly?" I asked. I had heard this somewhere, probably on TV.

"Yes, Charlie, some are. Shelters can be very good places, too, for people who need protection. But I'm an outdoor person and a little independent. When something like this happens, when you lose everything you own, you need to be around whatever makes you feel better."

"Like trees and space, right?"

The chief nodded. "You might say that."

I thought about what he had just said. It was scary to even think about losing everything.

"You weren't able to grab some clothes or a clock radio or anything?"

"No, Charlie. The water came up too fast, and I waited too long to leave. It's hard to leave your home."

I knew. I had run away once. My mom had thrown out my dead bird collection without asking permission. As soon as I left, I wanted to come back, which I did eventually. But first I walked to the edge of town and sat under a tree for three hours. There really was no place like home.

"Don't you have a family or cousins or someone?" I asked. It was none of my business, but I had been wondering about his family for some time.

The chief smiled, but he didn't seem like he was happy. "I have a sister, but we don't stay in touch. We haven't spoken for years."

"I've got a sister," I said. "And it's been years since we've been in touch."

"My sister is a very good person," said the chief.

"Mine is selfish and mean."

"That will change," he said.

"Not soon enough."

"When it comes to family, Charlie, especially sisters, you can't miss the forest for the trees. None of us is perfect. If you only see what you don't like about her, then you will miss seeing the things you do. That's a shame because those are the things that will bring you together and keep you a family, even when you're apart."

I've never understood that saying about the "forest for the trees." With an arborist using it now to talk about family, I was really confused.

"For the present, my only family is Pipe," added the chief. "Even he is living away from me now."

"At least he'll be warm," I volunteered.

"Yes. And it's only until we leave. I'm taking the little fellow with me. As much as we've been through together, I couldn't go without him."

I said, "So you're leaving before Christmas?"

He drank the last of his coffee. "Probably not. Pipe's shots and boarding set me back a bit, so I'm going to work another week or two. There's a chance for some overtime because my co-workers want time off. That'll help. I have nothing else to do on Christmas anyway. Might as well work."

Holiday music still played from the speakers. I looked at customers eating their burgers and fries. I looked at kids running around. None of them knew how close they were to a homeless man who lived in a tent and served fast food to pay for dog shots.

"That doesn't sound like much of a holiday," I said. "Working on Christmas and not even having Pipe."

The chief smiled and looked at his watch. He said, "Charlie, that's life. Sometimes, you have to bend in the wind."

Both of us stood up. He was talking about trees again.

"Well, I got to get back to work," he said.

"Yeah, I got to head home."

"Nice chatting with you, Charlie."

"Say hi to Pipe for me," I said as I left.

I had my facts. Pipe was in a shelter, and the chief was staying for Christmas.

That's when I decided about finding a tree and putting it next to his tent. A man who took care of his dog better than he took care of himself deserved a tree. So did an arborist who had to work at McDonald's on Christmas.

III

WHEN MY MOM SAW my puny tree, she forgot the true spirit of Christmas and lied.

"Charlie, it's so cute!" she exclaimed.

"Think so?" I replied.

"I see wonderful possibilities for a wreath here."

Mr. Paulson had said the same thing, but he didn't say "wonderful possibilities." My mom had other ideas, too.

"Maybe we could take some of its boughs and make a beautiful centerpiece for the table. You know what? Why don't we put pine needles in the crèche this year!"

Pine needles in our crèche? Jesus wasn't born anywhere near a pine tree!

Setting up the crèche was one of the few things I still did with my mom. Each year, I positioned the key players, including Mary, Joseph, and the inconsiderate innkeeper. My mom took care of the livestock, angels, and gawking shepherds. Early Christmas morning, I dropped the baby Jesus into his manger. She made sure straw was there to catch him. Over the next twelve days, I walked the Magi toward the stable. With me, they definitely took the long route. My mom made sure I didn't park them before Epiphany. She said it was a way for us to stay in touch with the true meaning of Christmas. She said people often forgot the miracle.

My mom always talked like that around the holidays. Now she wanted pine needles in the desert. Talk about miracles!

"Mom, I don't want to chop it up," I said about my tree. "I'm going to do something special with it." I didn't want to get more specific than that.

"Of course, dear," she said. "It's your tree. Just make sure you get it in some water so it won't dry out."

My mom had advice for everything. Most of it was good.

"If you plan on leaving it outside," she added, "please take care what you use for decorations. Things seem to be disappearing around here lately. Irene said one of Trudy's bowls was taken from the porch last week."

Trudy was Irene's pampered cat. She used to have two bowls, but I had given Pipe the other. I didn't know why a cat needed two bowls anyway.

"I'll keep an eye out for it," I replied. And I would.

"I just don't understand people," said my mom, shaking her head. "Christmas should be a time of giving, not taking. If you ask me, the world is an upside-down place."

I didn't say anything, but I knew she was right. A world where an arborist had to work at McDonald's to support himself and his dog while living in a homemade tent was definitely an upside-down place.

Before my tree went to the lot, I knew it would need a major makeover if it was to pass for a presentable evergreen. Grown-ups like to say that beauty is in the eye of the beholder. For a kid, ugly is always right there where you can see it.

So I borrowed my mom's rosebush clippers and carefully pruned the piney edges. On any Christmas tree, it's a tricky business. On a scrawny one, it's like reading your sister's diary without her permission. As soon as you start, you want to stop.

I couldn't do anything about the crooked trunk or missing top, but I picked away the gummy, orange ooze where the bark had been skinned. I put plenty of sugar in the tree water. My grandfather used to say that sugar was the best way to make a tree forget it doesn't have roots.

I thought of the chief as I fixed up the little tree, wondering if my work would meet his approval. Just my luck, the guy was an arborist. And not just any arborist. He was an arborist who said trees were his teachers.

Why couldn't he have been a car salesman or limo driver?

When it was time to decorate, I resisted borrowing from our own tree. Irene watched over our Christmas ornaments like she was guarding Fort Knox. She even knew how many blinking bulbs were in the light sets. She personally took charge of positioning every sphere and every star on every limb, as if the gravitational balance of the universe depended upon it. Einstein would have laughed. I know I did. There wasn't any way that I was going to sneak away with a major ornament.

So I settled for a handful of tinsel and the candy canes from my mom's mantle arrangement of angels looking down on Santa Claus in his sled. Believe me, candy canes didn't add anything to it. I popped two bags of microwave popcorn, which I strung together on several yards of dental floss. After that I threaded a garland of elbow macaroni. Then I found some construction paper and made a couple paper chains.

For the next two days, I worked as hard as any of Santa's elves. I gilded pinecones and glued glitter on acorns. I made clothespin reindeer and pipe-cleaner church bells. I constructed stars out of Popsicle sticks, and I cut Christmas trees from red felt. With the leftover yellow enamel from my go-cart, I painted a dozen light bulbs. I wrapped aluminum foil on Styrofoam balls, wired seashells, and readied frozen orange juice lids for hanging with fish hooks. When it seemed the ornaments were still lacking diversity, I added a couple of my CD-ROMs, which were scratched from a zillion plays. For the top, I found a cardboard angel left over from a Christmas pageant. Plastic wrap made it look glossy, and I glued it to an empty toilet paper tube for support. No angel was more down-to-earth.

When my mom observed my elaborate preparations, she said, "That's going to be quite a tree, dear. Have you decided where you're putting it?"

"Someplace," I answered, maintaining the mystery as politely as I could. After all, I couldn't really say that it was none of her business.

"Not around here," interrupted Irene.

My mom corrected her, "Irene, Charlie can put his tree wherever he chooses."

Irene rolled her eyes while I smiled. Mom had just silenced my sister, and I had just gotten the green light to move my tree wherever.

But the road to "wherever" had a pothole ahead. I had to get a fully decorated Christmas tree out of our house, past the neighbors, across town, and onto the lot.

Conjugating a Spanish verb in three tenses seemed easier. I considered the options. First, I could transport it—without any ornaments—by bike, and then decorate it at the lot. Even if I could decorate the tree in record time, half the town still might recognize me.

"Hey, isn't that the Roebecker boy over there hanging CDs on that poor excuse for a tree?"

The second option was to leave off the decorations and let the chief handle it. But that was like getting a Christmas card from your grandparents without any money inside.

What was the surprise in that?

Finally, I could boldly go where no boy on bicycle had gone before. I could deliver one upright Christmas tree that was already assembled and ready to admire.

Was there really any other choice for a kid who wanted to change the world?

It was a nerve-tingling marvel to see a fully loaded pine tree sitting atop my Mongoose BMX in the dimly lit secrecy of our garage on the morning of Christmas Eve. The sight of it tied to the steering tube with its crooked trunk wired to the handlebars gave me some serious goose bumps. I wondered if the first American in space felt this way just before launch. Was he ready to call the whole thing off, shimmy down the gantry, and go back to bed?

But the countdown had begun. If I didn't deliver it now, while my parents and Irene were out fighting the crowds of last-minute shoppers, and the chief was serving breakfast at McDonald's, then history would not be made.

Still, I hesitated.

Did making history have to be quite so obvious?

Then in one of those flashes a kid sometimes gets when he suddenly seems to be a genius, I ran back to my room, yanked the top sheet off my unmade bed, and returned to the garage. I carefully wrapped the sheet around the tree over and over again. When I finished, its needles had disappeared beneath a blue turban of cotton and polyester. It was an evergreen masquerading as a mummy. No ornaments would fall off now. No needles would be lost. More importantly, no one would know what I was carrying on my bike.

The next moment, I blasted out of our garage and down the street at a fast pedal. Mrs. Simon would have needed high-speed camera equipment to spy me from her window. I was a blur of blue.

At that clip, it only took a moment for me to realize I had aerodynamic issues that even NASA couldn't solve. My puny tree had suddenly met a hurricane. It was doing precisely what the chief said trees did—and taught us to do—even when wrapped in a sheet. It was bending in the wind. I didn't have any other choice but to slow down and grab my tilted passenger with one hand while I steered with the other. This saved it from falling, but it was the end of the blue blur.

I took the route where I was least likely to encounter familiar faces, including my parents. But I still drew my share of looks from curious pedestrians and passing motorists. I also snagged a decent double-take from a man stacking firewood. Kids pointed, too. It's a big deal seeing another kid take a Saturday morning to the edge, but I didn't see anyone I recognized. Not even Gooter.

As expected, no one was around when I reached the lot. I kept wearing my bike helmet as I unloaded the tree. Beneath the protective bowl of white plastic, one kid pretty much looks like another. I had brought bottled sugar water in my pack, and I had secured a coffee can to my bike rack.

My dad used the can when he changed oil in the Plymouth, but he'd never miss it.

I worked quickly. First, I braced the coffee can with stones so it wouldn't tip over. Next, I filled it with water. After unwrapping the sheet, I set the tree in the can and filled it with dirt so the trunk would stand straight. Finally, I inspected the ornaments. With the exception of flattened paper chains and tinsel stuck to the sheet, all trimmings, including the cardboard angel, had made it through the gale.

The chief's tree, heavy with swaying trinkets, stood at last in the middle of his well-swept campsite. If no one touched it and if the wind didn't blow, it might just stand through Christmas.

As I got on my bike, I turned for one last look. In the wide expanse of the lot, "puny" was truly the right word for it. More than ever, the little tree looked starved of something, but it certainly wasn't ornaments. Maybe it was the ugliest Christmas tree Irene had ever seen. Maybe it wouldn't stay upright for more than a day, but it was there, waiting for him. Like all gifts from the heart, it held a small promise.

That night, my mom prepared her usual Christmas Eve buffet of crab Newburg and Swedish meatballs served in her shiny chafing dishes. I could have managed with a hotdog and some tater tots, but my mom always got fancy on Christmas

Eve. At the table, she asked if I had put up my tree.

"Up and decorated," I answered, moving chunks of crab to the edge of my plate.

Irene started to say something, but she stopped herself. With major gift-getting only hours away, she may have decided to be nice to me and not push my buttons. She was really counting on that iPod.

"Where did you put it, son?" my dad asked.

"I donated it to a shelter," I replied, having prepared this truest of answers in advance. Chief Goodyear was in a shelter—his own.

Everyone stopped eating and looked at me. Irene's mouth was open.

"Why … how thoughtful of you," declared my mom. "I had no idea."

I shoveled a forkful of rice, as if I enjoyed it, and said, "After you told me about those rescue missions giving away turkey at Thanksgiving, I figured homeless people might want to have a Christmas tree, too."

My mom looked at my dad. Her eyes were beaming. My dad disconnected from his plate long enough to keep the ball in play.

"Well, that was a very considerate gesture, Charlie. Good job, son."

Naturally, you can't count on your parents to be satisfied with just the broad brushstrokes. They have to know about the paint under your fingernails, too.

"Which shelter was it, dear?" my mom asked, tilting her head. "The Crossroads?"

I couldn't lie on Christmas Eve, not with the baby Jesus already on his way to the manger, and definitely not over fancy buffet food like this. So I played dumb.

"I don't know its name, Mom," I replied. I looked in her direction, but not at her. "I just saw it from the bus. I think it's new."

My mom considered this response with a thoughtful expression. "That must be the shelter that just opened on Marsh Street," she announced. "I think the Evangelical Mennonites are running it."

I nodded, but I didn't say anything. Undoubtedly, Marsh Street was in the general neighborhood. And Mennonites of any kind were beyond my comment.

"It's important to think of others. Especially this time of year," said my mom. She turned to Irene and said, "Wasn't that nice of Charlie, Irene?"

Irene swallowed her food and said, "Oh, yes."

The way she said it made me look up. She was staring at me over her glass of cranberry juice. Her eyes had a message. Her next words seemed to speak in code.

"Charlie is very nice to strangers," she lilted. "Everyone says so."

I studied the crab on my plate, trying to disguise a sudden plunge into panic.

Did she know?

My dad said, "We'd do well to be nice to everybody, Irene, whether we know them or not."

Silence unfolded. I waited for Irene to say more. If she knew where my tree had gone and if she knew what I had been doing on the lot, now was the moment to tighten the noose.

For some reason, she didn't.

"I suppose," she agreed flatly. Somewhere in one of our closets, an unwrapped iPod was waiting for a nametag. Had Irene decided to not tempt Santa?

As we drove by the lot that night on our way to Mass, I stared at the chief's campsite out the window. There really wasn't a point in not looking. In the front seat, my dad focused on the road while my mom filled our pledge envelopes with money. Irene was looking out the window, too.

I spied the chief standing close to his grill, a shadowy figure with hands outstretched and being warmed over a red glow. I thought I recognized the silhouette of a teakettle on the grill and a ski hat on his head.

The chief's tent, the tires, and the tree were only shadows on the lot. I strained to catch a blink of tinsel or the shimmer off a CD, but I saw only darkness.

Irene suddenly nudged me.

"Don't worry, stupid," she whispered with a tenderness that surprised me. "I won't tell anyone about your ugly tree. Just be nice to me."

It snowed that night. It was only a dusting of powder, but those in our house who wished for a white Christmas woke to one. If it hadn't been for the chief sleeping in a tent, I would have wished for it, too. My dad said that the first snow is like a fresh start.

That morning, the only start that interested me was starting the Christmas joy. There was the baby Jesus to place in the manger and stockings to empty. Most urgently, there was a pile of gifts under our huge tree that was waiting to be opened. I didn't believe in Santa anymore, but I still believed you got what you asked for. I also believed in surprises.

I received plenty of both that morning. I made a killing in the action figure, card warfare, and electronic game departments. Naturally, Irene was happy with her new iPod.

Next came an onslaught of relatives, including several of my cousins with loot of their own. Amid the chaos of company, Christmas dinner, toy talk, and play, the day passed in a blur. Sadly, I didn't give much thought to the chief. I didn't worry about the snow melting on his tent. I didn't regret that he was working at McDonald's. I didn't wonder what he ate for Christmas dinner while I demolished baked ham. I didn't even think about the tree. I guess Irene was right when she said that I'm still a kid.

The day after Christmas, I awoke feeling like I had cheated in catechism class. I decided to make a couple ham sandwiches, pack them in aluminum foil, and run them down to the tent. Even the day after, Christmas ham was still Christmas ham. I also wanted to know if the tree had survived the night.

But my mom announced we were making an overnight to Thorndale to visit more relatives. What timing! I wanted to complain, but I couldn't say that travel was a terrible imposition on getting ham into the right hands.

In the Roebecker household, kids don't have votes, so, under protest, I went. But I called Gooter first to find out what he had gotten for Christmas and to tell him I wouldn't be over to play because I was being abducted. He gave me his list. Except for the clothes, all were quality gifts, including a new bike.

Then he said, "Hey, have you checked out the lot?"

I hesitated for a second, lining up the right words. "I've been too busy," I said.

"That homeless guy put up a tree right next to his tent. It's the ugliest tree you've ever seen. And he decorated it, too. You gotta see it. It's creepy looking."

"Really?" I said, not quite speechless.

"Yeah. We drove by yesterday. My mom stopped because she wanted to leave the chief some food. Christmas cookies or something. And there was this tree. I was going to get down and check it out. I mean, the thing looks like some kid decorated it. But my mom wouldn't let me. She said I had no business there. If you can believe that!"

I believed it. I had no business going to Thorndale, but orders were orders.

"Was the chief there?" I asked.

In the background, I heard Gooter's mother telling him to keep it short.

"No," he answered. His voice dropped. "I didn't see him. She left the food in the tent. I told her a crazy dog was tied up there, but when she got back to the car, she said there wasn't any dog. So maybe it ran away or got stolen or run over or something. Hey, I gotta hang up. Check it out when you get back, if it's still there. I don't think it will be because it's barely standing, apart from being ugly. My mom says merry Christmas and all that. Bye."

I put down the phone. Gooter had been a gold mine of information. The puny tree had made it through Christmas day, upright and decorated. The chief had gotten cookies. And now I knew that the other charitable soul was Gooter's mom.

Two days later, we were back from Thorndale. It hadn't snowed while we were gone, which was good news for the chief. But, as soon we hit town, Irene asked if we could go to McDonald's for lunch.

She didn't just ask. She pleaded.

"Oh, please, Daddy. Just this once." She was a drama queen in wool.

I thought my dad would hold fast to his principles, wanting to keep his perfect record intact. Just in case he wavered, I was quick to side with reason.

"Count me out. I'm not hungry," I said from the back. That drew silence, so I added, "Anyway, it's not good to eat too much fast food."

It was a quote from someone who actually worked at McDonald's, but I couldn't cite the source. My dad smiled at me through the rearview mirror, and that's when I realized he was going to compromise.

"I'll tell you what," he announced. "We'll use the drive-thru. How's that? Then I don't have to go inside."

I couldn't believe what Irene did next. She released her seat belt, and she reached across the front seat to hug my dad from behind. We never unbuckled while the Plymouth was in motion, and we never distracted Dad while he was behind the wheel. I waited for him to give the command to cease, desist, and buckle up, but he went along with the moment. He took his eyes off the road long enough to peck Irene on the cheek. My dad was definitely slipping. I figured it must be the holidays.

"Maybe I'll have a burger, too," he said.

"And I'll order a salad," my mom added.

"I'm going to have a spicy chicken sandwich with fries," declared Irene.

"Are you sure don't want something, Charlie?" my dad asked.

"I'm good," I answered grimly.

Mortified was more like it. Adding my order to the list

would only keep us parked outside McDonald's that much longer. I didn't want the chief, who was probably working the drive-thru window, to recognize me.

I imagined him poking his friendly face through the sliding glass, scanning the occupants of our minivan until he spotted me.

"Hey, Charlie, is that you?" Then he'd acknowledge my parents' dumbfounded looks with, "Hi there, folks. I'm Bill, a friend of your son. He's been keeping an eye on Pipe for me. Haven't you, Charlie?"

Their perplexed faces would ask, "Pipe? A pipe? Who? What was that?"

Or the nightmare might deepen. He would say, "Hey, Charlie, guess what? Someone brought a decorated tree to the lot."

I quickly scanned the car for something to hide behind. A two-page spread from our local paper, preferably the sports section, would have provided good coverage, but the best I could find was a shabby-looking Christmas pageant program that had been left over from the previous Sunday. It definitely wasn't something you could bury your face in—Hallmark cards were bigger—but it would have to do.

As we pulled into the drive-thru lane and approached the menu board, I shriveled into the far corner of our rearmost seat. The pageant program was touching my nose.

A man's voice took our order. With the microphone crackle in the background, I couldn't be sure if it was the chief.

My dad eased the Plymouth forward to the pay window. I shifted my weight, doing my best to disappear into the cup holder on my door. Words from the pageant program hugged my eyelashes.

"Joseph of Arimathea played by Jason Huo," I read. I could smell the ink.

The pay window opened.

"That will be $16.55, please."

Without microphone crackle behind it, I could tell that it was a young man's voice. It definitely wasn't the chief.

I peered over the program. My mom was handing money to my dad. From the window, a pale, hairless hand took it. I couldn't see a face. My dad's head was blocking the view.

We edged forward to the pickup window. Again, I tried to make myself disappear. I had met the chief at the pickup window before. Its wide glass opened into the frantic, employee-crowded McKitchen where practically anyone inside could see into the car. If I was to be spotted, it would be here.

I turned away, and pretended to be fascinated by the door lock. The pageant program was stuck to my face. Then I heard the glass windows slide open.

"Here we go," announced a peppy accent.

Yes. A girl!

At the sound of paper bags stretching around hot food, I began to relax. The smell of french fries flooded our car.

"And here are your drinks."

My dad took his time positioning the cups. He may not have set a foot inside the Golden Arches, but he was clocking plenty of overtime just outside them.

I wanted to nudge the Plymouth forward and make that window slip behind us. Out of the corner of my eye, I saw what appeared to be my dad popping a fry into his mouth.

Double time, Captain! March!

"Is there ketchup in the bag?" asked my mom.

This was no time to scream, but I wanted to. I could only hide and hope the chief wasn't hovering in the background with ketchup ready. My face was hot. For a moment, I wished I'd never seen the man or taken him a tree. It was a terrible wish.

"Happy holidays," cheered the girl in the window.

Then my dad accelerated. The window closed behind us. As we pulled onto the street, I dropped the program, sat up, and looked back. I was convinced I had just lived through the definition of a close call.

IV

I SHOWED UP AT THE lot early the next morning
with the ham sandwiches, but as soon as I reached
Hildreth's, I saw I was too late. No grill. No tires. No tent.
The chief had left.

He had been gone for at least a day, maybe more. Trash
had blown back onto the lot. The campsite wasn't swept. My
mortification at McDonald's had been for nothing.

The lot was vacant except for the tree. My tree … the
chief's tree … the ugliest Christmas tree … if you believed
Irene and Gooter. It was still standing, but the decorations
were gone. Only the tinsel was left.

The sight left me with a strange kind of emptiness, as if
one of my organs had suddenly gone missing. I felt like the
time our family dog got leukemia, and my dad took him
to the vet to be put down. It was that kind of emptiness.
The chief had left, and I had never gotten a chance to wish
him Merry Christmas or Happy New Year or say good-bye. I
hadn't even wished him a good life. A better life. Sometimes,
you can do only small things to fix a big problem.

When I got to the tree, I noticed something white stuck

between the pine boughs. At first, I thought it was paper snatched from the wind, but I saw handwriting and recognized the shape. It was an envelope.

I pulled it from the branches and read, "To Whomever Finds This."

The words were written across the front in dark ink. I flipped the envelope over. The flap was sealed.

Not everyone uses "whomever" in our town.

That was my first thought. Only those people who know when it's good grammar, and I'm not one of them. My second thought was a sixth-grade grasp of the obvious.

I, Charlie Roebecker, am the first whom on the lot to find it!

It was like a message in a bottle, except it had been waiting for me to come ashore. I fingered the flap, wondering if I should open it here. It seemed a strange business leaving behind an envelope for a whomever the writer would never know.

My gaze dropped to the tree. It looked shorter and punier. Without ornaments, it was scrawnier than ever. The tinsel only made it look more lonesome. I followed its crooked trunk to the ground, looking for my dad's coffee can, the one I left as a tree stand. It was missing. The big stones I had positioned there to brace it were gone, too. I stepped back, wondering how the tree was standing without them. Its trunk seemed to disappear into the ground.

Then I saw that it did disappear into the ground. The trunk was buried in the ground! Now I understood why the tree looked shorter. The chief had planted it.

"No way!" I exclaimed, immediately dropping to my knees for a closer look.

The trunk had been sunk up to its lowest boughs. The earth around it was tightly packed and molded into a round trough. The dirt in the trough was muddy brown. He had watered the tree, too!

It seemed like a lot of work for nothing. A Christmas tree couldn't grow after it was cut. It didn't have roots!

For as long as I could remember, I had watched our own Christmas trees dry up in the backyard after their unceremonious removal from our living room. I watched their needles turn orange-brown while we waited for the tree disposal man and his chipper to arrive in our neighborhood. Some things you just knew in this life—your name, the color of your mother's eyes, and what happened to a Christmas tree after Christmas.

I stood and tugged on a bough, expecting the tree to break loose and fall. Surprisingly, it resisted. It might have been my imagination, but it seemed to pull back.

I wondered if the chief had decided to apply his arborist's skills to a scrawny pine or if he simply had needed an empty coffee can for the trip. I looked at the unopened note in my hand, wondering if the answer was inside.

Slipping a fingernail under the flap, I tore it open and removed a folded piece of paper that I immediately recognized. It was the sign I had left in his tent before Thanksgiving, the one advertising the Safe Harbor Hospitality House lunch. On the blank side, a note filled the entire page. I stood next to the tree and read it:

If you are who I think you are, I have so many things I want to say beyond thank you. But I only have one side of this paper. So here's the short list. The sleeping bag was warm, and that sweater was priceless. (I love blue elephants.) The flashlight let me read, while the sewing kit saved my shorts. The oatmeal was delicious, those nuts were a treat, and I'm still taking the vitamins. That may be why I haven't gotten sick. Did you bring those cookies, too? As for our tree, it is the most beautiful Christmas tree anywhere and the most originally decorated. The angel is lovely. I've kept the trimmings for Christmases to come, but I've returned the little pine to the ground, where all trees belong. It seems fair that if I was given the opportunity to begin a new life after tough times, then why shouldn't it? Something tells me it will do well with you nearby. Water it, Charlie, when you can. (But no sugar!) You, too, will do well, wherever you end up belonging.

My jaw dropped. I didn't quite believe what I had read until I read it again. But there it was.

Water it, Charlie, when you can.

So he knew! Even about the sugar.

After all my precautions, he had found out somehow. Had he seen me? Had I left some clue? Had somebody told him? Gooter's mom?

I folded the note and started to put it in my pocket when I noticed handwriting at the bottom of the printed side. It was penned in the same ink.

PS: Be nice to your sister. She's not as bad as you think. In fact, she is a lot like you. She brought the socks and cat food. Mr. Hildreth saw you both.

Bill

That was one too many surprises for a kid just getting over Christmas.

Mr. Hildreth a spy? Irene a charitable soul? What next? A scrawny Christmas tree sprouting roots?

I stared at the note, amazed at how complicated a sister could be. She had called the chief creepy. She had wanted to bring the police. She had refused to pray for him. Then she had brought him socks. A contradiction seemed to be there, but it did explain why she had kept my secret. Now I'd have to keep hers. Helping the chief had become *our* secret.

I thought about saying something to her to let her know I

knew. I wanted her to see that I wasn't as dumb as she thought I was, but that wouldn't have been nice. Irene had told me to be nice to her, and the chief had written the same. I didn't think I had any choice now.

After refolding the note, I slipped it into my jacket pocket. Something inside me felt stretched and rubbery. It wasn't an awful feeling or even a nice one. Just new.

Then I biked home.

It snowed four inches of wet stuff that night. The next morning, Gooter called.

"Guess what?" he blurted.

"The chief's gone," I replied.

"You know the ... Huh? Who told you?"

"I went to Hildreth's."

"Really? My mom just got back from leaving him fudge. Make that not leaving him fudge. She said the lot was empty. Let's go build a fort."

"Meet you there," I said, knowing I didn't have a choice. If the snow hadn't messed with the puny tree, Gooter would.

I arrived first and saw that it was still standing. Being scrawny had its advantages in a snowstorm. There was hardly any tree for snow to stick to.

Gooter showed up wearing new winter boots.

He said, "Hey, there's that ugly tree I told you about. Isn't it pitiful?"

I was ready. "Yeah," I said. "I guess the chief left it for us."

Gooter looked at me and said, "What do you mean?"

"To take care of," I replied.

Now Gooter really looked at me.

"What are you talking about? It's dead. It doesn't even belong here. I say we pull it up."

"That's what homeless people do, Gooter."

"What?"

"They leave something behind."

"Get out!"

"It's like a gift for the people who help them when they're homeless—people like your mom who give them stuff."

Gooter stared at me. "You're kidding, right?"

Smiling, I said, "Yeah, but I think we ought to leave it, just in case."

Sometimes a friend needs help to see the right path.

"It'll dry up anyway," argued Gooter as we headed to the tree.

"I know," I said. "But does that mean we should knock it down?"

We stared at the tree. Gooter didn't answer. Instead he pulled on a bough, bending the trunk toward him. I watched and held my breath.

"It's going to be in the way when we play," he said, suddenly letting go.

"Maybe." I watched the tree snap back and stand straight

again. "But no one is playing ball anyway. What's the big deal?"

Gooter scooped a handful of snow, molded it, and moved away from me.

"I suppose," he said.

"I'd feel better if we just let it fall by itself. Let nature do it."

"Charlie, have you been talking to the reverend or someone? You seem awful worried about doing the right thing."

"No," I replied. "I just think that if people leave something behind and we don't know why, we better not mess with it."

"Okay. You're getting too complicated. Leave the stupid tree. I don't care."

Then Gooter threw a snowball at me, hard.

"Hey, no fair!"

"What do you mean no one is playing ball?" he said, grabbing another handful and swiftly making a new one. "Catch!"

I dodged it, scooped snow, made a quick one, and then unloaded. Both of us moved away from the tree, making war and laughing.

Later, we rolled snow boulders and circled them into a fort. I had the idea to build it around the tree, and Gooter quickly agreed.

"Yeah. So no one can see how ugly it is."

That's the way we left it. The chief's tree stood inside a snow fort, safe and unseen.

We took down our own tree, Irene's tree, on Epiphany. It was the same day I moved the Magi in our crèche into the final position next to the baby Jesus and that poor-looking stable. Even back then, accommodations for the homeless weren't much to look at.

A week later, the tree-chipper man stopped in our neighborhood. He dragged the tall Douglas fir to the street and pushed it into the wide mouth of his whirring machine.

I thought of the chief as I watched the tree get chewed into confetti, and I wondered what he would have said. Naturally, I found myself thinking a lot about him in those first weeks. I wondered if he had made it to Florida with Pipe. I wondered if he had found a job and a home. I wondered if he would plant old Christmas trees there, too.

A thaw in January melted our snow fort, making the chief's tree a public spectacle again. Still, no one but me paid any attention to it from the bus. Not even Gooter was interested. Turning twelve that month took over his brain. All he could talk about was becoming a teenager. It was awful.

I knew the melting snow would give the little tree plenty of water, but when I finally got to the lot, I saw that it might as well have been standing in the middle of a desert. It was drying up just like Christmas trees are supposed to. Its needles were turning rusty and barely hanging on. When I touched one of the boughs, a whole handful fell to ground. Nature may be slower than a chipper, but it gets the job done.

The chief had talked about trees being tough and teaching us stuff about surviving. He might have been right about the rooted ones, but a planted Christmas tree was far from that school.

Still, you had to give it credit for standing up. When the weather warmed up in February and we didn't get any rain, I did my duty. Every Saturday, I took a jug of (sugar-free) tap water to the lot and poured it on the puny tree. I did it because the chief had asked me to do it, not because I expected the scrawny little pine to rise from the tree grave. When one jug didn't seem enough, I packed more dirt around the chief's trough to make the dike higher so I could add two jugs.

By then, not a needle was on it. The chief's tree was a skeleton. It hardly had a shadow. Somehow, it managed to stay upright. Maybe the chief had done something tricky underground, a secret that only arborists knew. Defiantly, it braved a freak blizzard in early March. A windy St. Patrick's Day came and went. Still it stood. April brought rain and then mud. Grass started sprouting in the lot.

In May, the ground was dry enough to start baseball. The first Saturday, I got a call from Gooter saying the boys were meeting at Hildreth's to play. As soon as we got there, kids wanted to pull up the tree to clear the outfield. The general opinion was that the little tree was the ugliest dead tree on the planet.

Fortunately, it lined up perfectly with first base and home plate. When I suggested using it to mark our right field foul line, everyone rushed to verify the geometry, and then agreed.

Gooter was the first to yell, "Let's play ball!"

That summer, the chief's tree miraculously escaped annihilation. Somehow, it didn't get run over in our chase for pop flies and diving catches. Even hard ground balls bouncing foul didn't touch it.

Then school started again, and I didn't go to the lot. I occasionally looked out the bus window when we passed. Sometimes I even noticed the tree, but I wasn't thinking about it anymore. I guess time and turning twelve does that. A dead tree that a homeless man left in a vacant lot became one of those things that I hardly noticed. I hardly thought about the chief, either.

When the afternoons turned cool and the leaves started to blaze, we returned to the lot again to play soccer. This time, the tree became our corner marker. Amazingly, it stood in the perfect spot.

As it turned out, it was perfect for a good reason. If it hadn't stood where it did, then Ricky Martinez, our right forward and a kid with a keen eye for dropped pocket change, wouldn't have yelled, "Hey, come look at this!" one Saturday as he positioned the ball for a corner kick next to the tree. No one else would have noticed.

We gathered around him, following the tip of his finger where it pointed at the tree. All of us stared. Gooter and I dropped our jaws. Ricky was pointing to green. The tree bough closest to the ground was green! Pine tree green!

The chief's Christmas tree had baby needles.

"No way!" blurted Gooter, his eyes wide.

I stared, not quite believing it either. Then I took one of the upper boughs between my fingers and bent it. Instead of snapping, it wrapped around my knuckle. It was green on the inside, too.

"Good thing we didn't pull it up," Gooter said.

Everyone moved away. Ricky kicked the ball, and play resumed.

But I hung out near the tree. I wanted to jump up and down. I wanted to wrap my arms around it. But that would have looked funny in the middle of a soccer game. How crazy was a kid supposed to get over a Christmas tree that managed to rise from the dead?

Had that second jug of tap water saved it? Had leaving out the sugar helped? Had the hands of an arborist somehow made a difference? Or had nature pulled it off on its own?

While most trees were losing their green for the winter, the ugly little pine had sprouted it.

What a time to come back to life.

"C'mon, Roebecker!" shouted Gooter. "Quit playing with the stupid tree."

I turned to look at them. Like me, they were young and careless. I didn't know how I could say that I preferred the company I was keeping. I didn't know how I could say I was standing next to a phenomenon, one for the record books. I didn't know how I could tell them that Chief Goodyear, the homeless arborist who had camped where we were playing, had been right. Trees are tough.

I couldn't. So I ran into the game and kicked the ball.

Within a month, the tree was green again. Green, scrawny, and, according to Gooter, still ugly. But I didn't care. The teaching had begun. The chief might have said, "Charlie, welcome to tree school." Besides, I had been right from the start. You only needed imagination to see what this tree might become.

Our soccer games and my visits to Hildreth's lot ended when the ground froze and an early snow fell. Even though I still hadn't figured out how trees get by when the dirt freezes around them, I didn't worry about the little pine. I knew it would survive.

Christmas came. My dad drove Irene and me to Mr. Paulson's tent for the annual picking. Again, Irene chose another tree for the White House. It wasn't as tall as last year's, but it was horribly perfect. This time, I didn't make any comments about clones or steroids. I was nice. And she was nice back.

"Charlie, I want you to help me decorate it this year," she declared.

She actually said my name.

"Aren't you going to get one, too?" my father asked, nodding toward the corner where all the rejects stood.

"Yeah, Charlie, got some dandy lop-offs," agreed Mr. Paulson. "Won't charge ya."

I shook my head and said, "Thanks. I'm not doing a tree this year."

My dad might have thought I had lost my charitable side, but I hadn't. I just hadn't seen a homeless man camped out in a vacant lot in our town.

As usual, my mom and I set up the crèche, and she talked about miracles. When she asked me if I believed in them, I said I wanted to. Obviously, I kept the miraculous comeback of the tree at Hildreth's to myself. I wasn't sure if it was a miracle.

I thought a lot about the chief that Christmas. There were reports on the TV about the hurricane people. Some were going home, rebuilding, starting over, and spending their first Christmas in new houses. I wondered if the chief was among them. I watched the pictures on the news, looking for him and trying to pick out a man with a dog. But I never saw him. I would never know if he went back or if he found work in Florida helping knocked-over trees stand straight again.

The pine tree on Hildreth's lot did grow the next year. It grew greener, taller, and fuller. Most of the boys agreed that it wasn't quite as ugly as the year before.

Even though I didn't know it then, it would eventually grow so much that it would get in the way of the games we played. Its branches would interfere with corner kicks. Its piney top would knock fair balls foul. It would force us to retreat to real ball fields. By then, we would be big kids.

Mr. Hildreth eventually hung Christmas lights on it when the holidays arrived, running an extension cord from his store. His lot became our local Rockefeller Center at Christmas. Mr. Hildreth's tree became another holiday landmark, just like the sixteen thousand lights decorating the front of Billy Wetmore's house.

Eventually, the tree I had brought and the chief had planted grew into the tallest, fullest pine tree in the neighborhood. Eventually, no one noticed the crooked trunk behind the thick evergreen boughs. No one remembered its missing top. Eventually, people who were new to town stared and exclaimed, "Look at that tree! Isn't it beautiful?"

And that's the truth. I don't overdo my adjectives.